# A TALE OF ESCAPE

# A TALE OF ESCAPE

KENNETH HAINES

# CONTENTS

# ONE
## THE NIGHT OF THE ABDUCTION

### The Unseen Arrival

The air shimmered with an unsettling stillness, a stark contrast to the chaotic symphony of life that had filled the world just moments before. As the sun dipped below the horizon, casting an eerie glow across the landscape, the ground trembled slightly, not from an earthquake, but from the distant vibrations of something far more sinister. Those who looked up saw only stars; few noticed the darkened ship hovering silently above, cloaked in a veil of invisibility. It was a harbinger of an unseen arrival, one that would change the course of humanity forever.

In the quiet of the night, the first of the captives began to feel an inexplicable pull, a force urging them towards a fate they could not comprehend. One by one, they were drawn from their homes, their lives interrupted by a sudden flash of light that swallowed them whole. The sensation was not one of fear at first, but rather a strange curiosity, a sense of wonder mixed with dread. They were lifted from the earth, leaving behind the familiar comforts of their existence, unaware that they were to become spectacles in a cosmic zoo, mere exhibit pieces for the amusement of alien spectators.

Among the abducted was a young woman named Elara, whose life had just begun to unfold with the promise of love and adventure. As she materialized within the confines of the alien craft, the stark reality of her situation dawned upon her. She was not alone; others surrounded her, their faces a blend of confusion and terror. The walls of the spaceship were cold and metallic, a stark reminder that they were far from home, trapped in a realm governed by beings who viewed them as little more than exotic curiosities. Elara's heart raced as she scanned the faces of her fellow captives, each one reflecting a shared fear of the unknown.

As days turned into weeks, the aliens observed the captives with an unsettling detachment, studying their every move, their every interaction. Elara soon realized that she was not merely a prisoner; she had become part of an experiment, a test to determine compatibility with another species. With a young alien girl assigned to monitor her, the lines between predator and prey began to blur. The alien's gaze was both curious and calculating, as if she were assessing whether Elara possessed the qualities deemed necessary for a connection—an unsettling reminder that she was being watched, evaluated for her worthiness as a mate for the aliens.

Yet within the confines of their captivity, whispers of rebellion began to stir among the captives. United by their shared plight, they forged bonds that transcended fear, fueled by a desperate desire for freedom. Elara found herself at the forefront of this movement, her spirit ignited by the thought of escape. As she and her companions plotted their return to Earth, a flicker of hope blossomed in the darkness of their reality. They were no longer just animals in a cosmic zoo; they were individuals with a fierce resolve to reclaim their lives, to break free from the invisible chains that bound them, and to confront the unseen arrival that had changed their destinies forever.

A World Turned Upside Down

The darkness of space enveloped the ship, a stark contrast to the blue and green orb we once called home. It felt surreal, like a nightmare that held a cruel twist at its heart. Here we were, a collection of species, plucked from our lives, stripped of our identities, and thrust into a bizarre cosmic menagerie. The aliens, with their iridescent skin and multiple eyes, observed us with an unsettling curiosity, much like humans would watch wild animals in a zoo. We were no longer the masters of our own destinies; we had become mere exhibits in a grand, interstellar display, our lives reduced to entertainment for those who viewed us as lesser beings.

As days morphed into weeks aboard the alien vessel, the reality of our situation sank in. The ship, an amalgamation of strange technologies and incomprehensible designs, became our prison. We were shown off to delegations from distant worlds, each with their own peculiarities and tastes. Some viewed us with fascination, while others regarded us with indifference, as if we were mere curiosities. I often caught glimpses of fear reflected in the eyes of my fellow captives, a shared understanding that we were being studied, dissected, and judged. The sense of urgency for escape grew stronger with each passing day, yet the how remained elusive, buried beneath layers of despair and uncertainty.

Then, one fateful day, they brought her aboard—an innocent girl, no older than twenty, chosen as my potential mate. The aliens had devised this twisted experiment to see if a bond could form between us, a connection that would justify our existence in their eyes. She was terrified, and I could see the confusion in her gaze as she took in the strange surroundings and the equally strange beings who held us captive. I felt an overwhelming desire to protect her, to shield her from the horrors of this cosmic zoo, but I was just as trapped as she was, a pawn in a game played by forces far beyond our comprehension.

In those fleeting moments, we spoke in hushed tones, sharing our fears and hopes, trying to forge a bond amidst the chaos. Her laughter, though tinged with fear, was a sound I came to cherish, a reminder of the humanity we still clung to. We devised a plan, however shaky, to escape this nightmarish reality. Each day we observed the patterns of our captors, looking for weaknesses, for opportunities. The connection we began to form became our lifeline, a flicker of hope in the darkness, urging us forward against the odds stacked heavily against us.

As we plotted our escape, the ship itself transformed from a place of despair to a symbol of resistance. We were no longer mere exhibits; we were survivors, determined to reclaim our freedom and return to a world that had seemed so distant. The cosmic zoo would not contain us forever. With each passing moment, our resolve strengthened, fueled by the belief that somewhere out there, among the stars, we could find a way back home. Together, we would rise against our captors, our spirits unbroken, ready to fight for our lives and the essence of what it meant to be human.

# TWO
# LIFE IN THE COSMIC ZOO

Strange Creatures and Alien Eyes

In the vast expanse of the universe, where shadows dance between the stars, strange creatures lurk in the corners of alien worlds, their eyes reflecting a multitude of colors and emotions. These beings, often perceived as monstrous or bizarre, possess a depth of understanding far beyond our own. Their alien eyes, like windows to their souls, scrutinize us with a mixture of curiosity and disdain as we, the unwilling exhibits of this cosmic zoo, become the subjects of their fascination. The very essence of their existence is entwined with our own, as they observe us not just as specimens, but as reflections of what they could never fully comprehend.

As we were transported from our home, the familiar sights and sounds of Earth faded into a haunting memory. The sterile environment of the alien spaceship was a stark contrast to the vibrant life we once knew. We were herded into a cold, metallic enclosure, surrounded by beings that defied all logic, each possessing its own form of beauty and terror. With every glance from their alien eyes, I felt the weight of our predicament—a chilling reminder that we were mere animals in a gallery, stripped of our autonomy, and reduced to mere entertainment for those who had plucked us from our lives.

Among the other captives, I felt an unspoken bond forming, a shared understanding of our plight. We were not just victims; we were survivors, each of us wrestling with the fear and confusion of our alien surroundings. As we watched the strange creatures observe us, I began to notice the subtle ways in which their eyes conveyed meaning. A flash of empathy, a spark of amusement, or a flicker of indifference—each glance revealed layers of emotion I had never anticipated. It was a reminder that even in the depths of captivity, connections could still form, however tenuous, and hope remained a flickering flame amidst the darkness.

Then came the moment that would change everything. From the shadows of the ship, they brought forth a young girl, no older than twenty, her wide eyes filled with wonder and fear. She was to be my mate, chosen from Earth to bridge the divide between our worlds. I could sense the weight of the experiment upon us, the scrutiny of the alien observers looming like a storm cloud. As she stood before me, I felt an inexplicable pull—a connection that transcended the barriers of language and species. In that fleeting moment, I realized that we were not just subjects of study; we were potential allies in a struggle for freedom.

As the days turned into nights in this cosmic cage, we plotted our escape. The alien eyes that once seemed so threatening now fueled our determination to break free from our confines. Our shared experiences, our silent conversations, and the bond we forged in the face of adversity became our greatest weapon against the forces that sought to contain us. Together, we would challenge the narrative imposed upon us, defying the very essence of what it meant to be a part of this alien zoo. The stars above whispered promises of freedom, and as we braced ourselves for the inevitable confrontation, we knew that our fight was not just for survival, but for the reclamation of our identities as beings worthy of dignity and respect.


## The Rules of Our Captivity

The rules of our captivity are etched into the very fabric of our existence aboard this alien vessel. Each day, we awaken in our glass enclosures, a stark reminder of our status as specimens rather than sentient beings. We are treated like rare animals on display, with the cold, watchful eyes of extraterrestrial visitors observing our every move. They document our interactions, our emotions, and even our most private moments, as if we are mere exhibits in a cosmic zoo. The aliens have established a hierarchy within our group, creating divisions that foster competition and distrust among us. It's a strategy to keep us subdued, forcing us to forget the unity we once shared on Earth.

Every detail of our lives is governed by unspoken rules that dictate our behavior. We are expected to perform for our captors, showcasing our intelligence and capacity for emotion. Those who resist are met with harsh consequences; an eerie silence fills the air when one of us is taken away for punishment. The aliens thrive on our fear, relishing the control they wield over us. Our days blend into one another, filled with a monotonous routine designed to strip us of our individuality. We learn to mask our true feelings, to play along with the performance that keeps us safe from further scrutiny.

Yet, within this suffocating environment, we find whispers of rebellion. Some among us have begun to communicate in secret, speaking in hushed tones about escape. We share our dreams of freedom, of a world beyond the confines of this ship. The desire to return to Earth fuels our determination, igniting a spark of hope in our hearts. We form bonds, realizing that together we are stronger than we could ever be alone. The connections we forge become our lifelines, reminding us of who we are and what we are fighting for.

As if to mock our plight, the aliens introduce a new element to our captivity: a young woman, no older than twenty. She is brought aboard seemingly to be evaluated for compatibility with one of us—a twisted experiment in love and connection. Her presence adds a layer of complexity to our situation, as we grapple with the implications of her arrival. We are both drawn to her and wary of the attention she attracts from our captors. The aliens observe her interactions with us, recording every glance and moment of connection, as if our fates hinge on her acceptance or rejection.

In the shadow of these rules and this strange new dynamic, we find ourselves at a crossroads. Will we succumb to the despair of our circumstances, or will we harness our shared humanity to spark a revolution? The cosmic zoo may seek to cage us, but our spirits are resilient. We understand that breaking free from our captors requires not just an escape plan but a profound transformation of our mindset. Together, we will challenge the very rules of our captivity, refusing to be mere animals in their display, and instead reclaiming our right to be the authors of our own destinies.

# THREE
# UNDERSTANDING OUR CAPTORS

## The Language of the Stars

The language of the stars was not one of words but of silence, an eerie stillness that enveloped those who found themselves ensnared within the confines of the cosmic zoo. The shimmering constellations above were a stark reminder of the vastness beyond our planet, yet they felt hauntingly indifferent as we became mere specimens on display. Each twinkling light was a distant witness to our plight, a harsh contrast to the alien eyes observing us from the shadowy corners of their ships. In this otherworldly menagerie, we were stripped of our humanity, reduced to curiosities to be studied and judged.

As I stood among my fellow captives, the remnants of our former lives echoed in our conversations. We spoke in hushed tones, sharing tales of our homes, our dreams, and the mundane joys of existence that now felt like distant memories. We were not only fighting for survival; we were clinging to our identities. The language we shared was laced with desperation, woven with threads of hope that one day we would break free from this cosmic confinement. Yet, the stars above, indifferent as they were, seemed to mock our attempts to communicate our shared humanity.

When they brought her aboard, the young girl with bright eyes and an unwavering spirit, it felt like an intrusion into our fragile world. She was a living embodiment of a connection we had longed for, yet I could sense the weight of expectation on her shoulders. The aliens had chosen her as a subject of observation, a potential mate for me, hoping to witness the sparks of attraction that could ignite between us. She stood there, bewildered and frightened, her presence a flicker of warmth in the cold, metallic abyss of the ship. I found myself drawn to her, but the circumstances of our meeting felt more like a cruel experiment than a genuine encounter.

As days turned into weeks, the tension between us grew palpable. The aliens watched our every interaction, their inscrutable faces revealing nothing of their intentions. I longed to reach out to her, to bridge the chasm that separated us, but fear held me back. Would I be merely another specimen in their twisted collection, or could we forge a connection that transcended the cold calculations of our captors? The language of the stars was a silent witness to our struggle, yet in our hearts, we began to develop a dialect of our own, one filled with unspoken emotions and shared glances that spoke volumes.

In the quiet moments, as we stole glances at the stars outside, I felt the stirrings of rebellion within me. We were not just animals to be caged and studied; we were beings with the capacity for love, connection, and resistance. The language of the stars, once an emblem of our captivity, became a rallying cry for survival. It was a reminder that while we might be trapped in this cosmic zoo, our spirits could not be contained. Together, we began to weave a plan, our whispered words forming a tapestry of hope that would guide us toward freedom, one star at a time.

## The Purpose Behind the Captivity

The purpose behind the captivity of humanity transcends mere curiosity; it is a reflection of the complexities of existence, the nature of power, and the inherent desire to understand what lies beyond the familiar. In a universe teeming with life, humans are not unlike the wild animals captured for display in a zoo. The alien species that have taken us from our home do not merely seek to observe us; they aim to study our behaviors, our relationships, and ultimately, our essence. This captivity serves as a grim reminder of our vulnerability in the face of the vast unknown, where we are reduced to mere subjects of scrutiny in an intergalactic exhibition.

As we languish within the confines of this cosmic zoo, the aliens engage in a form of observation that is both unsettling and enlightening. They have stripped us of our autonomy, yet in doing so, they have inadvertently revealed the depths of our interconnectedness as a species. The way we respond to our surroundings, to each other, and even to the moments of despair and hope speaks volumes about our innate resilience. The captors watch with a clinical detachment, measuring the nuances of human emotions, relationships, and the indomitable spirit that drives us to seek freedom, even in the darkest of circumstances.

The introduction of a young girl, chosen for her potential to connect with one of us, adds another layer to this complex dynamic. In her, the aliens see the opportunity to explore the intricacies of companionship and love, emotions that are often deemed as weaknesses by those who wield power. The connections formed in captivity become a focal point of their study, as they seek to understand whether love can flourish in an environment designed for control and observation. Her presence revitalizes hope within the group, sparking a longing for autonomy and the possibility of forming genuine bonds, despite the oppressive circumstances that surround us.

While the experience of captivity is fraught with despair, it also ignites a fire of resistance within us. The desire to escape is not merely a yearning for freedom; it is an assertion of our identity, a declaration that we will not be reduced to mere specimens for entertainment. The cosmic zoo may have stripped away our physical freedom, but it cannot extinguish the spirit that drives us to dream of liberation. Each moment spent plotting an escape serves as an act of defiance, a reminder that we are more than the sum of our captors' observations. We are beings of complexity, capable of love, hope, and rebellion.

Ultimately, the purpose behind our captivity serves as a catalyst for self-discovery. In the face of alien scrutiny, we are forced to confront our vulnerabilities and strengths, to redefine what it means to be human in a universe that often views us as curiosities. The experience compels us to reflect on our values, our relationships, and our innate desire for connection, even under the most arduous conditions. As we navigate this harrowing journey, we find that the true essence of our existence lies not in our captivity, but in our relentless pursuit of freedom, understanding, and the bonds that unite us as a species.

FOUR

THE GIRL FROM EARTH

A New Arrival

The air in the enclosure felt thick with anticipation, a palpable tension that echoed the fear and confusion swirling in my mind. I watched the stars flicker through the transparent walls of the spaceship, each twinkle a distant reminder of the world I had known. The metallic hum of the craft was unsettling, a sound that vibrated through my bones, reminding me of my captivity. What had begun as a scientific curiosity had morphed into a nightmare, one that felt all too real as I grappled with the knowledge that we were nothing more than specimens to these aliens. They had stripped us of our freedom, and with it, our identity.

It was then that she arrived, a sudden intrusion into my already disoriented reality. The alien mechanism that brought her to our enclosure was both awe-inspiring and terrifying. One moment, I was staring into the endless void of space, and the next, there she was—a young woman, no older than twenty, her wide eyes reflecting the same bewilderment I felt. She seemed fragile, almost ethereal, yet there was a spark of resilience in her gaze that caught my attention. I observed her as she took in her surroundings, her breath hitching as she realized the gravity of her situation. I could not help but wonder about the circumstances that had led to her being plucked from Earth, just as I had been.

The aliens watched from the shadows, their intentions clear. They were not merely interested in our survival; they sought to study our reactions, to gauge the chemistry between us. It felt surreal, the idea of being evaluated like some romantic experiment. My heart raced at the thought of forging a connection with someone who was as much a prisoner as I was. I felt an undeniable urge to reach out to her, to bridge the chasm of fear that separated us. In that moment, I realized that our shared captivity could spark a bond, one that transcended the boundaries imposed by our captors.

As days passed, we navigated the delicate dance of curiosity and caution. We exchanged glances laden with questions unasked, our movements constrained by the watchful eyes of our alien captors. I learned her name was Elara, a name that resonated with a promise of hope. Each encounter brought a glimmer of understanding, a shared acknowledgment of our plight. In the confines of the cosmic zoo, we found solace in conversation, recounting tales of our lives on Earth, dreams we had nurtured, and the simple joys that had been stripped away. The connection between us deepened, a flicker of defiance against the oppressive forces that sought to keep us apart.

In the quiet moments, when the stars glowed softly against the dark expanse, I realized that our escape would not only be a physical act but a journey of the heart. Together, we could find a way to resist the fate the aliens had imposed upon us. As we plotted our escape, I felt a surge of determination. Our connection was a lifeline, a beacon guiding us through the darkness.

No longer would we allow ourselves to be mere exhibits in a cosmic zoo; we would reclaim our freedom, our lives, and each other. In the depths of despair, love blossomed—a force powerful enough to challenge the very fabric of our captivity.

The First Encounter

The moment the light enveloped me, I felt an overwhelming sense of dislocation, as if the very fabric of reality had been torn apart and stitched back together. The hum of machinery and the flickering of strange luminescent panels surrounded me, and I could barely comprehend where I was. My heart raced as I took in my surroundings. I was no longer on Earth; I had been pulled into something beyond my wildest fears. The cold, sterile environment felt alien, with walls that seemed to pulse with a life of their own. In that instant, I understood that I had become a specimen, something to be observed and studied by beings who found amusement in our existence.

As I gathered my thoughts, the first encounter with my captors unfolded before me. Shadows shifted and morphed into forms I could barely recognize. They were tall and slender, with skin that shimmered in hues I had never seen. Their eyes, large and unblinking, were windows into a consciousness that felt both curious and dispassionate. They observed me with a clinical detachment that sent chills down my spine. I was an exhibit in their cosmic zoo, a mere curiosity to be scrutinized and cataloged, stripped of my humanity. In that moment, the reality of my new life settled in like a heavy cloak; I was no longer the master of my fate.

Days passed in a blur of surreal encounters, interspersed with the unnerving sensation of being watched. I was introduced to other captives, beings from distant worlds, each with their own story of abduction and loss. The air was thick with shared despair, yet a glimmer of hope flickered in the unlikeliest of places. We exchanged glances, words unspoken but understood, forging bonds that transcended our differences. Together, we began to plan our escape, igniting a spark of rebellion against our alien captors. It was here, amidst the shared pain and desperation, that I first felt the stirrings of connection with one of the others—an unexpected ally who would change everything.

The day came when they brought her in, a young girl who resembled the visions of freedom I had clung to in my darkest moments. She was fragile but fierce, her eyes filled with a determination that mirrored my own. The aliens seemed intent on observing this interaction, as if they believed we could somehow bridge the chasm between our worlds. I watched her, my heart thundering as unspoken words lingered in the air, a palpable tension that hinted at the possibility of something more profound than mere survival. Here, in the heart of this cosmic cage, the notion of connection blossomed like a wildflower in the most barren of landscapes.

As we navigated the challenges of this bewildering existence, our bond deepened, fueled by an unwavering resolve to escape the confines of our captors. Each moment spent together was a reminder of what we were fighting for—not just our freedom, but a chance to reclaim our lives, our identities, and our humanity. The cosmic zoo had stripped us of so much, yet in each other, we found the strength to resist. As we plotted our escape, we became more than mere specimens; we were warriors of our own fate, ready to confront the unknown and reclaim the stars that had been mercilessly taken from us.

FIVE

## BUILDING A CONNECTION

Moments of Fleeting Hope

In the dimly lit enclosure of the cosmic zoo, moments of fleeting hope flickered like distant stars, teasing the inhabitants with the possibility of freedom. Each day, the strange lights of the alien spacecraft above served as a reminder of the life that existed beyond the glass-like walls of our prison. Among the captives, there was a shared understanding that hope was a fragile thing, easily crushed by despair, yet it was also a lifeline we clung to in the darkest hours. We whispered tales of a world we once knew, a planet vibrant with life, where we had roamed freely under the sun, unburdened by the weight of captivity.

When the aliens first brought us aboard, we were bewildered creatures, thrust into an unforgiving reality. Many of us had been taken from our homes without warning, as if we were mere specimens to be cataloged and studied. As we adapted to our new surroundings, we began to notice the small moments that ignited our spirits. A shared laugh among fellow captives, a glimpse of the stars through the enclosure's ceiling, or the unexpected kindness from a passing alien curator could momentarily lift our hearts. These fleeting moments reminded us that we were still alive, still capable of feeling joy amidst the shadows of our existence.

Then came the day when they introduced her—the girl who would be my companion, chosen seemingly at random from the earth they had invaded. She arrived with a mixture of confusion and fear, her eyes reflecting the same sense of entrapment we all felt. Yet, in the fleeting glances we shared, I saw a spark of recognition, a connection that transcended the barriers of our circumstances. It was a reminder that, even in this bizarre tableau, a bond could form, igniting a flicker of hope that perhaps we could escape together, that we could reclaim our lives from the clutches of our captors.

As days turned into weeks, we navigated the complexities of our shared captivity. The girl, with her laughter and warmth, became a beacon in the suffocating darkness. We began to communicate in secret, exchanging stories of our pasts and weaving dreams of a future beyond the cage. Those stolen moments, where we envisioned a life free from alien eyes, filled us with the strength to resist the despair that threatened to engulf us. With every shared secret and whispered plan, the cage felt a little less confining, and hope surged like a tide within us.

In the end, it was those moments of fleeting hope that fueled our resolve to escape the cosmic zoo. We became more than just specimens; we were rebels, dreamers, and lovers, bound by the desire for freedom. Each heartbeat resonated with the promise of a future where we could reclaim our identities and fight back against our captors. Hope, though ephemeral, became our most potent weapon, reminding us that even in the depths of despair, the stars were still within reach, waiting to guide us back home.

## The Language of Emotion

Emotions are the heartbeats of our existence, the threads that weave through our experiences, connecting us to one another and to the world around us. In the confines of the alien ship, a dazzling and terrifying spectacle of advanced technology and foreign beings, these emotions take on an even greater significance. The sense of fear is palpable, a weight pressing down on every soul within the glass enclosure. We are not merely specimens on display; we are vessels of longing and despair, our emotions laid bare for our captors to scrutinize. Every flicker of hope or pang of sadness resonates through the ship, echoing in the vastness of space, creating a language that transcends the barriers of species.

As the aliens observe us, they witness the nuances of our interactions—the laughter shared between friends, the silent glances exchanged between lovers, the tears shed in moments of vulnerability. Each reaction becomes a lesson, a study in what it means to feel. In their eyes, we are not just humans; we become embodiments of emotion, a living gallery of the joys and sorrows that define our existence. They catalog our responses, intrigued by our capacity to love, to grieve, to hope. In their quest to understand us, they may overlook the depth of our experiences, reducing our complex emotions to mere data points in their cosmic research.

Yet within this alien gaze lies a profound irony. While we are studied like animals in a zoo, our emotions serve as a form of resistance. Each time we connect with one another, each act of kindness or defiance, we reclaim a piece of our humanity. We resist the labels imposed upon us and remind ourselves that we are more than just exhibits. When the young girl appears, plucked from her life on Earth, the weight of her presence adds another layer to this intricate tapestry of feeling. Her bewilderment mirrors our own, and in her vulnerability, we find a spark of connection. It is this shared experience of being thrust into the unknown that ignites a flicker of hope, a reminder that even in captivity, we can forge bonds that defy our circumstances.

The language of emotion speaks not only of suffering but also of resilience. In the face of uncertainty, we learn to communicate beyond words, expressing our fears and desires through gestures, glances, and moments of silence. The young girl, observing us, becomes a part of this unspoken dialogue. Her presence is both a reminder of what we have lost and a beacon of what we might regain. As we navigate our strange new reality, we find ourselves drawn to her, a tether to the world we once knew. In her eyes, we see reflections of our own longings, a desire for connection that transcends the confines of the alien zoo.

Ultimately, the language of emotion is a powerful force, one that can challenge our captors' understanding of us. It is a reminder that we are not mere specimens to be studied but individuals with rich inner lives, capable of forging connections even in the most oppressive of circumstances. As we stand together in the face of the unknown, we embrace our emotions, allowing them to fuel our determination to escape this cosmic cage. In doing so, we transform our captivity into a story of resistance, survival, and the enduring power of human connection.

# SIX

# OBSERVATIONS AND EXPERIMENTS

## The Alien Watchers

The Alien Watchers were not just observers; they were the architects of our captivity, beings of unimaginable power who had transformed our world into a vast cosmic zoo. As they surveyed the Earth, they took pleasure in the diversity of life that thrived here, treating us not as fellow sentients but as mere specimens in their grand collection. Each day, they would glide silently through the skies, their immense ships cloaked in shadows, monitoring our every move, cataloging our behaviors, and taking notes on our interactions. With an insatiable curiosity, they scrutinized our laughter, our fears, and the way we formed connections, all part of an experiment that neither we nor they could fully comprehend.

Among the many species they had collected, humans were a particularly fascinating subject. Our emotions, our complexities, and our capacity for love and despair intrigued the Alien Watchers, who had long since lost the ability to feel in the same way. They reveled in our stories, our struggles, and our triumphs, dissecting them to understand what made us unique. Yet, beneath their cold, analytical gaze was a darker intent. They sought to find a mate for me, a young girl they had teleported from Earth, who would inevitably be pitted against me in a twisted game of cosmic matchmaking. This experiment was not just about observation; it was an exploration of connection that felt more like a cruel joke than a genuine inquiry into our nature.

The girl appeared in the confines of our enclosure, bewildered and frightened, her eyes wide with confusion. She was the embodiment of hope for the Alien Watchers, a potential bond that could form between us as they studied our interactions. I watched her from a distance, grappling with a torrent of emotions. Was I to see her as a companion or a rival? The stakes were high, for the Watchers were relentless in their scrutiny, recording every glance, every hesitant smile, and every moment of silence. I could feel their gaze upon us, an ever-present reminder that our fates were not our own but rather entwined in the whims of these extraterrestrial overseers.

As days turned into weeks, the tension within the enclosure grew palpable. The girl and I began to communicate, sharing whispers of our dreams and fears. In the shadows, I could sense the Watchers growing restless, their interest piqued by our burgeoning connection. Were they truly interested in the bond we formed, or were they simply eager to pull the strings of our lives for their own entertainment? The possibility of escape loomed over us like a specter. If we could find a way to break free from this celestial cage, we might reclaim our autonomy and defy the very beings that sought to control us.

In the midst of our struggles, a plan began to take shape. The Alien Watchers may have been powerful, but they underestimated the strength of our human spirit. With every passing day, the desire for freedom ignited a fire within us, fueling our determination to resist the fate they had laid out. Together, we would forge a path to liberation, not just for ourselves, but for all the beings trapped within this cosmic zoo. As we forged a bond against the odds, we began to understand that our true strength lay not only in our individuality but in our shared humanity, a force that could challenge even the most distant of stars.


## The Pressure of Expectations

In the vast expanse of the cosmos, expectations weigh heavily on those who find themselves trapped in unfamiliar circumstances. For the humans aboard the alien ship, this pressure manifests in myriad ways, shaping their daily realities as they navigate the strange new world around them. Each day, they are acutely aware of the eyes upon them, the alien spectators who view them not as individuals with hopes and dreams, but as mere specimens in a cosmic zoo. The weight of their predicament is compounded by the knowledge that their every action is scrutinized, leading to a sense of inadequacy that permeates the air like a thick fog.

The expectations set by their captors are not only external but also internal. The individuals aboard the ship grapple with their identities, torn between the instincts of survival and the desire to maintain their humanity. They feel the pressure to conform, to display behaviors that might win the approval of their alien observers. This internal struggle can be excruciating, as they attempt to navigate the fine line between embracing their true selves and performing for an audience that views them as curiosities rather than equals. The burden of expectation leads to an existential crisis, forcing them to confront the essence of what it means to be human in a world that seeks to define them otherwise.

Among the group, a young woman becomes acutely aware of the implications of these expectations when she is chosen to connect with a human male who has also been captured. The aliens, in their quest to understand human relationships, place her under immense pressure to form a bond that may not exist. This experiment of sorts leaves her feeling like an unwilling participant in a game where the stakes are both personal and profound. The expectation to connect, to feel something genuine, weighs heavily on her heart, creating an internal conflict that is both frightening and isolating.

As days turn into weeks, the pressure intensifies. The young woman observes her fellow captives, each one responding differently to the demands placed upon them. Some retreat into themselves, rejecting the expectations altogether, while others attempt to play along, often at the cost of their mental well-being. The alien zoo becomes a microcosm of societal pressures, where the fear of failure looms large. They are not merely fighting for survival; they are battling against the expectations that threaten to strip them of their individuality and reduce them to mere subjects of observation.

Yet, amid this turmoil, a flicker of resilience emerges. The young woman realizes that while the pressure of expectations is daunting, it does not have to define her. The connection she seeks with her fellow captive may not be dictated by the aliens but can emerge from genuine interactions and shared experiences. In this realization, she finds strength, choosing to embrace her humanity rather than conform to the roles assigned to her. The pressure of expectations may still linger in the background, but it no longer holds the same power over her spirit. Instead, she embraces the idea that true connection, forged in authenticity, can transcend the confines of the cosmic zoo, igniting a spark of hope in their shared struggle for freedom.

SEVEN

# THE PLAN FOR ESCAPE

## Gathering Allies

In the dimly lit confines of the alien ship, the atmosphere was thick with uncertainty and fear. The humans, scattered like forgotten toys in a vast cosmic zoo, huddled together, their eyes reflecting the flickering lights of the control panels. They were not merely captives; they were a fragmented community thrust into a nightmare beyond comprehension. As whispers of rebellion began to circulate, a feeling of hope ignited among them. It was clear that the only way to survive and perhaps reclaim their freedom was to gather allies, to forge connections in the most unlikely of circumstances.

Among the captives was Lena, a spirited young woman whose fiery determination shone even in the darkest moments. She understood that they were not just victims of an alien experiment but potential agents of their own fate. Lena took the first step, uniting those around her with shared stories of their lives on Earth. Each tale, filled with laughter, love, and loss, wove an invisible thread of solidarity among the group. In the heart of the cosmic cage, bonds formed like a tapestry, each person adding their unique colors to the collective struggle against their captors.

As the days turned into weeks, the group became more than just a collection of frightened individuals. They began to strategize, pooling their skills and knowledge to devise a plan for escape. Some were engineers, others artists, and a few had backgrounds in biology. Each person contributed in their own way, crafting ideas and solutions that might help them break free from the alien zoo. Lena spearheaded these efforts, her passion and charisma drawing others into the fold, instilling a sense of purpose that transcended their dire situation.

However, the constant presence of their alien observers added a layer of complexity to their plans. The young girl, a seemingly innocent spectator brought from Earth, became a focal point of their strategies. The others speculated about her purpose, wondering if she was a mere pawn in the aliens' game or if she held the key to their salvation. Lena approached her cautiously, seeking to understand her role while gauging whether a connection could be forged. The girl's eyes, filled with confusion and empathy, hinted at possibilities that could transcend the boundaries imposed by their captors.

As alliances formed and trust deepened, the group's resolve strengthened. They were no longer simply waiting for the day they would be returned to Earth; they were actively seeking a way to reclaim their lives. Gathering allies, sharing burdens, and fostering connections became their way of resisting the cage in which they found themselves. The cosmic zoo was not just a place of captivity; it transformed into a crucible for hope and defiance, where each moment became a step toward not just survival, but a powerful rebirth.

## Mapping the Zoo

The vast expanse of the alien spaceship resembled a twisted reflection of Earth, a haunting collage that mirrored our world while distorting its essence. Every corner of the ship was meticulously designed, echoing the structure of a zoo, but on a cosmic scale. Transparent barriers held us captive, separating us from the various species that had been plucked from their homes, much like how we capture wild animals for our own amusement. The walls vibrated with the whispers of creatures from distant galaxies, each possessing stories and histories that intertwined with ours in this desperate existence. Here, we were not just prisoners; we were exhibits, our lives scrutinized and analyzed by beings whose eyes were filled with a mixture of curiosity and indifference.

As I wandered through the various sections of the ship, I realized that each area was tailored to showcase the unique traits of the species contained within. The alien architects had crafted environments that mimicked the natural habitats of their captives, yet these simulations failed to capture the essence of true freedom. Instead, they served as a reminder of what we had lost. I could see a group of humanoid beings in a neighboring enclosure, their expressions a mix of fear and resignation. It struck me that we were all part of an elaborate performance, forced to put on a show for our captors, while the true horror of our situation lay just beneath the surface.

Our captors, resembling a blend of insect and reptilian features, conducted their observations with a cold precision. They would often teleport individuals from our enclosure to their viewing chambers, where they monitored interactions and emotions, searching for connections that could bridge the gap between species. I watched in anguish as they brought forth a young woman, barely twenty, to be a potential mate for me.

The moment she appeared, an unsettling mix of hope and despair surged within me. Would she be a kindred spirit, or merely another pawn in this cruel game? The weight of expectation hung heavily in the air, a tangible thread that bound our fates together in this cosmic zoo.

Days turned into weeks, and the oppressive atmosphere of the ship began to wear on us. The routines of captivity were punctuated by moments of unexpected camaraderie among the confined. We shared stories of our lives on Earth, our dreams, and our fears, crafting a fragile network of support that helped stave off the debilitating loneliness. The young woman, whom I had come to know as Lila, became a beacon of resilience amidst the despair. Together, we began to devise a plan for escape, fueled by our shared determination to reclaim our freedom. We were no longer mere animals on display; we were survivors, and we would not succumb to the whims of our captors.

As we plotted our escape, the ship itself transformed from a prison into a map of possibility. Each section held secrets we could exploit, each barrier became a potential path to freedom. The alien technology that surrounded us, once a symbol of our captivity, now presented an opportunity for liberation. We understood that we would need to act swiftly and decisively, for time was not on our side. The stars outside our window no longer felt distant; they were our destination, our hope. In that moment, we became more than just a pair of species brought together under duress; we became partners in a quest for freedom, ready to defy the forces that sought to keep us caged among the stars.

# EIGHT

# THE BREAKOUT

## Timing the Escape

The clock was ticking, a relentless reminder of the urgency that enveloped our every waking moment. As I sat in the dimly lit confines of the spaceship, staring at the shimmering void outside, the realization dawned on me that time was not merely passing; it was slipping away. We had been part of this cosmic zoo for far too long, our lives reduced to mere exhibits for the alien spectators. The plan for escape had taken shape in hushed whispers and stolen glances, but every second spent in this metallic cage felt like an eternity. I had to act quickly, for the longer we lingered, the more risk we faced of becoming permanent residents in this otherworldly menagerie.

In the days leading up to our intended escape, I meticulously observed the patterns of the alien guards. Their routines, though alien in nature, held a certain rhythm that I learned to anticipate. I noted when their vigilance waned, when their eyes glazed over in boredom, and when they seemed to engage in their own distractions. It was during these moments of inattention that I realized we could make our move. Timing was everything; a split second could mean the difference between freedom and confinement. I shared my findings with the others, a ragtag group of fellow captives who had endured the same torment, and together we forged a plan that pulsed with the promise of liberation.

The night before our escape, a palpable tension filled the air. I could feel the weight of our collective hope and fear, a mixture that threatened to crush us under its enormity. Among us was the young girl, the one chosen by the aliens to observe me, to determine if there was a connection worth nurturing. In the dim light of our cell, I caught her eyes, filled with a mix of curiosity and fear. I wondered if she understood the stakes at play, if she felt the same longing for freedom that coursed through my veins. With every passing hour, I felt a bond forming between us, a silent understanding that transcended our circumstances. Perhaps, in our shared desire for escape, we could find strength together.

As the hour approached, adrenaline surged through me. I could hear the distant hum of the ship's machinery, a constant reminder of the world beyond our prison. We huddled together, counting down the moments until we would put our plan into action. My heart raced as I recalled the final steps: disable the containment field, navigate the labyrinth of the ship, and reach the escape pod that would take us back to Earth. The weight of our plight rested heavily on my shoulders, but I was unwilling to let fear dictate my actions. It was time to reclaim our lives, time to break free from the chains that bound us.

When the moment finally arrived, we moved as one, driven by the shared hope of freedom. Every heartbeat echoed the urgency of our escape, every sound amplified in the stillness of the night. We slipped through the shadows, our hearts pounding in sync as we navigated the ship's corridors. As we approached the escape pod, I felt a surge of determination, knowing we were about to take our fate into our own hands. The alien zoo had underestimated our spirit; they had not accounted for the resilience of those who are desperate to be free. This was our time, our moment to defy the odds and reclaim our place among the stars.

## Facing the Unknown

In the heart of the vast cosmos, facing the unknown becomes an inevitable part of existence for those who find themselves trapped within the confines of an alien zoo. The cold, sterile environment of the spaceship was a stark contrast to the vibrant colors and sounds of Earth. Each day unfolded with a mix of fear and curiosity as we, the unwilling exhibits, grappled with the reality of our situation. The bright lights, the strange sounds, and the distant whispers of beings from worlds far beyond our comprehension filled the air with an unsettling energy. We were no longer the masters of our fate; we were merely animals in a cosmic menagerie, observed and studied by eyes that were alien to us.

As we pondered our fate, the arrival of the young girl added an unforeseen complexity to our existence. She appeared one day, seemingly plucked from Earth, and teleported into our midst like a fleeting dream. Her wide eyes held a mixture of innocence and confusion, reflecting our own as we tried to understand her purpose among us. Were we to be her companions, her subjects, or something more? The unknown stirred within us a blend of hope and despair. Would a connection form between us, or would we remain isolated in our shared captivity? Each moment spent with her raised questions that hung heavily in the air, thickening the atmosphere with unspoken fears.

The desire to escape became a shared dream among us, an ember igniting our spirits in the face of hopelessness. We exchanged glances filled with unyielding determination, recognizing that survival depended not just on our bodies but on our minds and hearts as well. As we watched the girl, we felt an urge to protect her, to shield her from the same fate that had befallen us. In those fleeting moments, we discovered a bond that transcended the boundaries of species, a connection forged in the crucible of shared adversity. It was in our whispered conversations and secret glances that we found solace, a reminder that we were not alone in this struggle against the unknown.

We began to strategize, our minds racing with thoughts of freedom and resistance. Every observation by our captors became a potential opportunity. The aliens, in their arrogance, underestimated our resilience and our capacity for ingenuity. We started to decipher their routines, learning when the guards would be distracted and how to exploit the weaknesses in their surveillance systems. The unknown no longer felt insurmountable; instead, it transformed into a canvas on which we could paint our escape. Armed with the hope of returning to Earth, we plotted our course, each step fueled by the desire to reclaim our lives.

Facing the unknown is not merely about the fear of what lies ahead; it is about embracing the possibility that exists within uncertainty. The girl, once a stranger, became a symbol of our shared humanity, igniting a fire within us that refused to be extinguished. Together, we would confront the dark abyss of our predicament, resilient against the cold gaze of our captors.

The cosmic zoo had confined us in body, but it could not cage our spirits. As we stood united, ready to face whatever awaited us beyond the confines of our prison, we understood that the unknown was not just our enemy; it was also a realm filled with potential and the promise of freedom.

NINE

THE JOURNEY HOME

Through the Void

Through the void, darkness enveloped everything, an endless expanse that stretched beyond comprehension. The ship, a metallic leviathan, glided silently through the cosmos, its occupants encased in a surreal stillness. I often wondered if this sensation was akin to what an animal felt while being transported in a cage, unaware of its fate, unaware of the eyes that watched intently from the shadows. The cold, sterile environment of the alien craft served as a constant reminder of our captivity. Each breath I took felt weighted by the knowledge that we were nothing more than specimens to be paraded before alien worlds, our very existence reduced to a mere exhibit.

The crew of extraterrestrial beings, with their shimmering skin and multiple eyes, studied us with an unsettling curiosity. They communicated in a language that resonated like a chorus of haunting melodies, their intentions often lost in translation. We were gathered together, a motley crew of humans—every one of us plucked from our lives on Earth. Some were terrified, while others clung to hope, believing in the possibility of escape. But the reality was stark; we were trapped within the confines of this cosmic zoo, where the stars outside the viewing portal felt more like a distant dream than a reality we could touch or grasp.

Among us was a young woman, perhaps twenty years old, whose presence stirred something deep within me. She was a spark of life amidst the despair, a reminder of what it meant to be human. The aliens appeared particularly fascinated by her, their attention unwavering as they observed her interactions with the rest of us. I felt their probing gazes as they scrutinized each laugh, each smile, and each fleeting moment of connection we shared. It was as if they were orchestrating a grand experiment, testing the bond between us, seeking to understand if love could thrive even in the most unnatural of circumstances.

As days turned into weeks, I began to formulate a plan. The thought of escape consumed me, a flickering flame amidst the darkness. I gathered others who shared my resolve, those who longed to break free from this alien menagerie. We whispered our intentions in the dead of night, plotting our course through the labyrinthine corridors of the ship, a ticking clock reminding us that time was not on our side. The young woman became my anchor, her spirit igniting a fierce determination within me. I knew that if we were to find our way back to Earth, we would need to harness that connection, to draw strength from one another.

The moment finally arrived when we seized our chance. An unexpected power fluctuation sent the ship into disarray, alarms blaring as the crew scrambled to regain control. We rushed through the ship, our hearts pounding in unison, fueled by adrenaline and the sheer will to survive. As we navigated the alien landscape, I glanced back at the young woman, our eyes locking in a silent promise. We would not remain caged any longer. Together, we forged ahead through the void, determined to reclaim our humanity and return to the stars from which we had been so cruelly taken.

## Trials and Tribulations

In the dimly lit confines of the alien ship, a sense of unease permeated the air. The metallic walls hummed with a foreign energy, and the low growl of machinery echoed like a distant thunder. We were not just prisoners; we were exhibits placed on display for the amusement of beings who regarded us as little more than curiosities. Trials awaited us, both physical and emotional, as we grappled with the reality of our situation. Each day felt like an eternity, filled with the harsh reminder that we had been plucked from our world, much like animals captured for a zoo, only to be shown off to creatures who marveled at our very existence.

Among the others, I found solace in shared stories of our lives back on Earth. Our collective memories became a refuge, a way to preserve our humanity in the face of overwhelming odds. Yet, as we recounted tales of laughter and love, the gravity of our captivity weighed heavily. Each laugh echoed hollowly in the alien atmosphere, a stark reminder of the joy that had been stripped away. We were not just facing the physical hardships of confinement, but also the emotional toll of being cut off from everything we held dear. The trials of survival were compounded by the longing for home, a bittersweet ache that gnawed at our spirits.

Then came the day when the aliens, in their insatiable curiosity, decided to conduct their own experiment. They sought to breed a connection between us and a young woman they had also brought aboard. She seemed barely old enough to understand the gravity of her situation, teleported into our midst as if she were an object rather than a person. I felt an overwhelming sense of protectiveness toward her, for she was thrust into a reality that mirrored our own fears. The aliens observed us closely, their cold eyes scrutinizing our every interaction, measuring the depth of our connection as if it were a commodity to be traded.

As the days turned into weeks, we found a sense of camaraderie within our group. We concocted plans to escape, whispering under the cover of darkness, sharing ideas that felt both daring and desperate. Each plan brought with it a glimmer of hope but also the weight of potential failure. The trials of our captivity became a crucible, forging bonds that transcended our circumstances. We shared dreams of freedom, of racing across the fields of Earth, unencumbered by the chains of our captivity. The thought of escape fueled our determination, igniting a fire within us that refused to be extinguished.

With every passing moment, we grew more resolute. The trials and tribulations we faced only strengthened our resolve to resist the fate laid out before us. We were not mere animals for display; we were individuals with hopes, fears, and dreams of our own. Together, we dared to imagine a future beyond the cold metal confines of the cosmic zoo. In our hearts, we nurtured the belief that even in the darkest of places, the spirit of resistance and the yearning for freedom could never truly be extinguished. As the stars beyond the cage beckoned, we knew that our story was far from over.

# TEN

# RETURN TO EARTH

## The Familiar Yet Strange Land

The air crackled with an unfamiliar energy, a blend of wonder and fear as I stepped into the vast chamber of the alien ship. The walls shimmered like liquid silver, pulsating softly with hues of blue and green that seemed to breathe in unison with the rhythmic hum of the vessel. It was a strange yet oddly comforting sight, invoking both curiosity and a deep-seated dread. This was a land I had never known, a reality that felt both familiar and utterly foreign. The creatures that roamed the ship were unlike anything I had ever seen, their forms twisting and bending in ways that defied the laws of nature I once knew. I was a captive in their cosmic zoo, an exhibit for the universe to behold.

As I wandered through the corridors, glimpses of other humans trapped within their own enclosures haunted me. Each face told a story of despair and longing, mirroring my own. We were not merely specimens for study; we were individuals, each with our own dreams and memories. Yet, the aliens observed us with an unsettling fascination, as if we were rare animals in a cage, stripped of our dignity. I felt a pang of sorrow for my fellow captives, as the weight of their hopelessness pressed upon my chest. The silence was deafening, interrupted only by the occasional whisper of an alien discussing our behaviors, analyzing our every move.

Then came the moment when they introduced the young girl, a mere twenty years old, chosen from the remnants of my world. She was a delicate creature, her wide eyes filled with confusion and fear. I could see the flicker of recognition in her gaze as she scanned the strange environment, searching for something familiar amidst the chaos. I felt an inexplicable connection to her, an urge to protect and guide her through this nightmare. The aliens watched closely, eager to see if any bond would form between us, as if our shared plight could ignite a spark of hope in the dark abyss of our reality.

In those moments, we became more than just specimens in a cosmic zoo; we became allies in resistance. Our whispered conversations turned into plans of escape, fueled by the burning desire to reclaim our freedom. We shared tales of our lives on Earth, of laughter and heartbreak, of the mundane beauty that once surrounded us. Each memory we recounted brought us closer, weaving an invisible thread of solidarity between our souls. It was a fragile connection, yet it gave us strength, transforming our fear into determination.

As we plotted our escape, the land we traversed became both a prison and a sanctuary. The strange beauty of the ship, once a source of fear, began to feel like a canvas upon which we could paint our rebellion. We were not just animals being paraded for entertainment; we were humans, resilient and capable of defying the odds. The familiar yet strange land of the alien ship would not be our end; it would be the backdrop for our fight for freedom, a testament to our unyielding will to survive and reclaim our place among the stars.

## Adjusting to Freedom

Adjusting to freedom was not merely about the absence of physical restraints; it was a profound transformation of the mind and spirit. After years of captivity aboard the alien vessel, the overwhelming sensation of liberation flooded through me like a tidal wave. The metallic scent of the spaceship was replaced by the fresh, earthy aroma of the world I had once known. Yet, amidst the exhilaration of newfound freedom, a lingering anxiety clung to me. The freedom I craved was intertwined with the memories of confinement, and even in the open air, I felt the ghosts of my past haunting every step I took.

The first days after my escape were spent in a daze, my senses overwhelmed by the vibrant colors of the landscape and the sounds of life that had flourished in my absence. I walked through the familiar streets of my city, now transformed by the passage of time. Trees swayed gently in the breeze, children played in the parks, and the laughter of friends echoed in the distance. Yet, the joy of reunion was tinged with an unsettling realization: I was no longer the same person who had left. My experience in the cosmic zoo had changed me, etched scars of fear and resilience into my very being.

As I navigated this new reality, the presence of the young girl brought by the aliens loomed large in my mind. She was a mystery—a symbol of the experiment they had conducted in their cold, calculating way. I had watched her from afar, her innocence juxtaposed against the backdrop of my trauma. The aliens had hoped to observe a connection between us, a bond that might signify something deeper. Yet, in my heart, I harbored an unsettling blend of curiosity and dread about what that connection could mean. Was she a potential companion, or merely another pawn in their game?

In time, I began to understand that adjusting to freedom also meant confronting these complexities. I sought solace in nature, allowing the rustle of leaves and the gentle flow of water to guide my thoughts. Each moment spent in the embrace of the wilderness helped me reclaim my sense of self. I realized that true freedom was not only about escaping the physical constraints of the spaceship but also about liberating my emotions and confronting the lingering shadows of my trauma. I needed to find my voice again, to reclaim my narrative from the hands of those who had sought to control it.

The journey toward healing was not linear, and the scars of my past were reminders of the struggles I faced. Yet, the hope of connection with the girl offered a glimmer of light amidst the darkness. As I ventured into the world, I felt a growing determination to forge my own path, to shape my destiny free from the influences of my captors. The stars that had once felt so distant now seemed like a map of possibilities, guiding me toward a future where I could redefine what it meant to be free. Adjusting to freedom was about reclaiming my identity, my agency, and ultimately, my place among the stars beyond the cage.

# ELEVEN
# THE AFTERMATH

## Reconnecting with Humanity

In the vast expanse of the cosmos, where the stars shimmer like distant memories, a profound sense of isolation can envelop those who have been taken from their home. No longer tethered to the earth, the humans found themselves trapped in a strange interstellar menagerie, a spectacle for alien eyes. This dislocation from their origins stirred a deep yearning within them, a desire to reconnect not only with their humanity but also with the fundamental essence of what it meant to be alive. Each day in the cosmic zoo became a reminder of their past, a past filled with laughter, love, and the warmth of shared experiences. Yet, in the face of their captivity, a flicker of resilience sparked within them, urging them to reclaim their lost identities.

Amidst the alien observers, the humans discovered that their shared plight forged an unbreakable bond. Conversations erupted in hushed whispers during stolen moments of respite.

They shared stories of familial love, childhood dreams, and the mundane joys that once filled their lives. This communion became a lifeline, a means of preserving their humanity in an environment designed to strip it away. The laughter that echoed through the cold metal confines of the spaceship was a testament to their indomitable spirit. Even as they were paraded like curiosities, they chose to celebrate their existence, reminding each other that they were more than mere specimens in a cosmic zoo.

The arrival of the young girl, brought to assess the possibility of a connection, stirred a whirlwind of emotions within the captive humans. She represented a beacon of hope, an embodiment of the future they yearned to reclaim. As they observed her innocence juxtaposed against their own harrowing reality, they felt an overwhelming urge to protect her, to share with her the beauty of humanity that had not yet been tainted by the chilling grasp of alien captivity. In her presence, they found a flicker of life that reignited their own desires, reminding them of the deep bonds that could exist between individuals, even in the face of unimaginable circumstances.

Yet, the challenge remained: how could they nurture this connection while ensnared in a web of alien scrutiny? The humans devised subtle ways to communicate their emotions and intentions, weaving a tapestry of understanding that transcended language and culture. They found solace in shared glances, quiet gestures, and the unspoken promise of solidarity. Each moment spent with her was an act of defiance, a refusal to be mere exhibits in an alien showcase. They knew that if they could instill in her the essence of their humanity, they could ultimately reclaim their identities and inspire her to be a conduit for their liberation.

Reconnecting with humanity became not only a survival

tactic but a revolutionary act. The humans realized that their stories, their laughter, and their love were powerful tools against the cosmic forces that sought to diminish them. In that alien zoo, they cultivated a garden of hope, where the seeds of friendship and resilience could flourish against the odds. Their ultimate escape would not merely be a physical journey back to Earth; it would be a reclamation of their spirits, a return to the essence of who they were as a species. As they began to weave their experiences into the fabric of the universe, they understood that the true power of humanity lay in its ability to connect, to love, and to resist, no matter the cage that held them.

## Haunted by the Stars

The stars hung above like distant, cold eyes, watching us with a judgment that felt ancient and unyielding. We were no longer the masters of our fate, but rather mere specimens in a cosmic zoo, plucked from our home planet to be exhibited before eyes that were not our own. The vastness of space became a cage, and each twinkling star transformed into a spotlight, illuminating our every move. As I stood among my fellow captives, I could feel the weight of their despair, a shared understanding that we were caught in a web of alien curiosity. The grandiosity of the universe felt mocking; how could such beauty exist while we languished in confinement?

Our captors, these enigmatic beings from distant worlds, were fascinated by our humanity. They studied our emotions, our behaviors, as though we were rare animals in a traveling zoo, observed from behind glass walls that separated us from their world. They would watch as we interacted, taking notes on our laughter, our fights, and our tears. They were particularly interested in our connections, the bonds we formed, and how love might blossom in such dire circumstances. It was as if they were trying to decipher the depths of our souls, probing for the essence of what it meant to be human.

One day, a strange event unfolded that threw our fragile existence into further disarray. A young girl, no older than twenty, materialized in our midst as if summoned by the very stars that had betrayed us. She was a living embodiment of the hope we had nearly abandoned, yet her arrival felt like a cruel twist of fate. The aliens observed her with keen interest, eager to see if a connection would spark between her and one of us. It was a terrifying thought, to be reduced to mere subjects in an experiment, but the possibility of companionship ignited a flicker of rebellion within my heart.

As days turned into weeks, the girl and I forged a bond that transcended our bizarre circumstances. We found solace in whispered conversations under the artificial light of our captors, sharing dreams of freedom and escape. Each stolen moment was a rebellion against the reality we faced, a testament to our resilience. The aliens, with their clinical detachment, continued their observations, unaware that the very connection they sought to exploit was becoming a force of resistance against our plight. In our shared laughter and quiet conversations, we began to reclaim our humanity, turning the sterile environment of the cosmic zoo into a backdrop for our burgeoning love.

Haunted by the stars, we plotted our escape from this otherworldly captivity. The very essence of our struggle served as a reminder that even in the darkest of places, hope could thrive. As we became more daring, we found ways to communicate with others who shared our fate, igniting a collective spirit of rebellion. The aliens may have captured our bodies, but they could never cage our spirits. Together, we would rise against the confines of our existence, turning the cosmic zoo into a battleground for our freedom, determined to reclaim our place among the stars, not as exhibits, but as the rightful inhabitants of our own world.

TWELVE
A NEW BEGINNING

## Finding Purpose

In the dim light of the alien enclosure, the concept of purpose became a haunting echo, reverberating through the minds of those who found themselves trapped in a cosmic zoo. The stars had once filled us with wonder and dreams of exploration, but now they served as a reminder of the vastness beyond our cage and the stark reality of our captivity. As we were paraded before the cold, unfeeling gaze of extraterrestrial beings, understanding our purpose became essential. It was not merely about survival; it was about reclaiming our dignity, our humanity, and ultimately, our identity.

Each day brought a new challenge to our spirits as we navigated the alien landscape, filled with creatures who viewed us as curiosities rather than sentient beings. In this strange world, the essence of our existence was put to the test. We were more than mere specimens; we were the culmination of generations of hopes, dreams, and experiences. Finding purpose in this twisted reality meant recognizing that even in the face of dehumanization, we still had the power to connect with one another, to nurture the bonds that tethered us to our home. It was through these connections that we began to forge a sense of resilience, a collective determination to resist the fate that had been thrust upon us.

As the weeks turned into months, the arrival of a young girl brought an unexpected twist to our narrative. She was a living embodiment of hope, a reminder of what we had lost and what we could still fight for. The aliens had chosen her as a potential mate for one of us, but in her presence, we discovered a deeper purpose. We became her protectors, her allies in a world that sought to exploit her innocence. Our focus shifted from merely surviving to nurturing the spark of humanity within her, and in doing so, we rekindled our own sense of purpose.

We began to communicate in ways that transcended language, sharing stories of our past, our dreams, and our fears. Each interaction with her reinforced our resolve to escape this cosmic prison. Our purpose was no longer just about individual survival but about creating a future that could honor our shared humanity. We realized that our existence in this alien zoo was not just a lesson in despair but also an opportunity to redefine what it meant to be human. We would not allow ourselves to be mere exhibits; we would fight to reclaim our narrative.

In the end, finding purpose became an act of defiance, a testament to our spirit as a species. The stars that once seemed so distant now represented our ultimate goal: freedom. Each moment of connection, each act of resistance, and each decision to stand against our captors reaffirmed our right to exist as more than mere animals in a cage. Our purpose was intertwined with the fate of those we loved, and we were determined to break free, to reach for the stars not as prisoners, but as the authors of our own destiny.

## The Bonds We Forge

In the chilling expanse of the cosmos, the bonds we forge transcend the limitations of our earthly existence. As we found ourselves ensnared in the clutches of our captors, the alien beings who had taken us from our home, we quickly learned that survival hinged not just on our individual strength but on the connections we nurtured among one another. Each of us, plucked from our lives, was thrust into a terrifying realm where the familiar faded into the background, replaced by the stark reality of being an exhibit in a cosmic zoo. In this strange place, we discovered that our shared experiences—fear, confusion, and a longing for freedom—formed the foundation of our resilience.

The moments we spent together became a sanctuary amidst the chaos. We shared stories of our lives on Earth, of laughter and love, and of dreams still lingering in the corners of our minds. Those narratives wove a tapestry of hope, reminding us of who we were before the stars had become our prison. As we gathered in dimly lit corners of the alien ship, our voices would rise in unison, creating a symphony of humanity that echoed through the cold metal corridors. In the face of our captors' indifference, we found strength in unity, bolstered by the knowledge that we were not alone. Each bond we forged became a lifeline, a tether that kept our spirits alight in the darkest moments.

The arrival of the young girl, summoned to determine the viability of connection between us, added another layer to our collective struggle. She was not just a pawn in the aliens' cruel game; she represented a flicker of hope, a chance to reclaim what had been stolen from us. As we observed her, each of us felt the weight of responsibility grow. We were not only fighting for our own freedom but also for hers. The desire to protect her fueled our determination, and her presence became a catalyst for our growing bonds. The question loomed large in our minds: could love bloom amidst captivity? The potential for connection, once mere whispers in the dark, now surged with newfound urgency.

As we navigated the complexities of our situation, the bonds we formed extended beyond mere companionship. They transformed into a fierce camaraderie, an unspoken commitment to one another's survival. We exchanged knowing glances that spoke volumes, strategizing and plotting our escape in hushed tones. Each shared meal, every laugh and tear, solidified our determination to break free from the chains that bound us. The connections we developed became a source of power, a reminder that even in the face of overwhelming odds, together we could defy the fate that had been thrust upon us.

In the end, it was the bonds we forged that would lead us to freedom. The strength we drew from one another became our greatest weapon against the alien forces that sought to keep us subdued. As we stood together, ready to face the unknown, we understood that our connections were the essence of our humanity. They reminded us that even in the darkest corners of the universe, love, friendship, and solidarity could shine brightly, illuminating our path to escape. In an existence that sought to diminish us to mere specimens, we chose to rise, united in our quest to break free and reclaim our destinies among the stars.

www.ingramcontent.com/pod-product-compliance
Lightning Source LLC
Chambersburg PA
CBHW061640130726
47996CB00003B/1394